CONTENTS

A Strange Scent

CHAPTER 1

EARTHQUAKE!

Lassie sniffed at the odd-looking footprint in the crisp snow, curled back her upper lip, and snarled.

"What's the matter, girl? Pick up the scent of something you don't like?" Corey Stuart, the Forest Service's most famous district ranger, patted the collie on her aristocratic head, then crouched beside her. He quietly peeled off one of his fur-lined gloves and traced the track's outline with his forefinger. "Wolverine!" he exclaimed.

Lassie whined with distaste, even though she had never met up with a wolverine.

"Nothing to worry about, old girl!" said Corey with a chuckle as he straightened up. Shuffling back

"Wolverine!"

and forth in his snowshoes in order to ward off the biting cold, he added, "Come on, let's find a sheltered spot where we can bed down for the night, away from the blizzard force of this Alaska wind! Remember, this is the first day of my vacation, and I want to start off fresh tomorrow after a good night's sleep."

High overhead, the droning of a small twin-engined airplane rattled through the late afternoon air.

Plane Overhead

Corey tightened the thongs under the hood of his parka and squinted upward. It was no use. He couldn't detect the outline of the plane because of the heavily swirling white clouds. As he narrowed his eyes, the words, "I still think you're out of your head!" crackled from the depths of one of his parka's deep pockets.

Corey chuckled, removed the walkie-talkie from the pocket, and held the mouthpiece to his lips.

Corey Uses His Walkie-Talkie

"Hello, Ace? This is Mobile Two speaking. Why do you think I'm out of my mind, my bush pilot friend?"

"Because you should go to Florida on your week off, and toast that leathery hide of yours under the scorching sun! But not you! You get a seven-day leave, and what do you do? You ask me to fly you into the wildest section of Alaska, so you can pick out potential sites for new wilderness areas!"

Ace Answers

The plane sputtered out of ear-
shot in the distance, but the pilot's
voice continued to transmit loud
and clear. Ace continued, half in
exasperation and half in admira-
tion, "Corey, I couldn't keep up
with you when we went through
forestry school together, and I *still*
can't keep up with you!"

"Don't forget to pick me up in
a week!" replied the ranger as the
plane dropped below the clouds and
dipped a wing. "You should be able

"So Long!"

to land on the frozen riverbed at Bear Skull Point."

"You'd better be waiting for me, chum," answered Ace Dawson. After a slight pause he continued, "I'll have to sign off now. I'm hitting a lot of turbulence up here, and it's all I can do to keep this featherweight kite airborne!"

Corey laughed softly and slipped the walkie-talkie back into his cavernous pocket. "Come on, Lassie. Let's hit the trail!"

"Let's Go, Lassie!"

Lassie trotted along at his side as Corey slogged forward through the snow like an oversize Eskimo. She didn't care where she was, as long as she was with *him*. If he had wanted her to accompany him across the burning Sahara, she wouldn't have given it a second thought. Her only wish was that she could help carry something— either that enormous pack that sagged on his back, or the Mossberg 800 rifle slung over his shoulder.

They Slog Forward

As if reading her thoughts, Corey remarked, "I'd let you carry this rifle, girl, but I think you'd find it uncomfortable."

Lassie snuggled her head against his side.

"You'd better not run off and do any exploring! If the Tlingit Indians see you, they'll either pop you into a stew pot or use you as a sled dog!"

The collie barked happily and plunged into a snowbank. White

Lassie Plunges into a Snowbank

clouds scattered in all directions.

Fifty yards behind Corey and his companion, a squat brown beast perked up its stubby ears and listened to the dog's barking. Then it grunted hungrily. No flesh had crunched between its jagged teeth since it had torn the carcass of a caribou calf to shreds a week earlier. It was about to plod forward once more in search of food, when the earth shook violently beneath its feet.

A Silent Observer

"Lassie! It's an earthquake!" shouted Corey, pitching face forward in the snow as the ground buckled upward beneath. Deafening grinding and scraping sounds smashed against his ears. It seemed as though the shaking earth were groaning in rage. Hundreds of tree trunks lurched in one direction, then snapped in the opposite direction, while underground rocks violently shifted position.

The bewildered collie careened

Earthquake!

against a splintered tree trunk, then tumbled head over heels against a rocky hillside which was splitting open like a stone sandwich. Bulging upward through the scattering rocks was what appeared to be an enormous mound of black hair.

Corey staggered unsteadily to his feet. He was unable to stand completely upright because one of his snowshoes had been crushed. Impatiently kicking the broken

"Hang On, Girl!"

snowshoe to one side, he turned his head in search of his beloved canine friend. "Girl! Are you all right?"

Lassie, cautiously sniffing at the mass of black hair uncovered by the newly opened hillside, wagged her bruised tail and barked. *She* was all right, but what was this strange thing she was exploring?

"Well, I'll be!" exclaimed the husky ranger, sucking in his breath. "It's the frozen body of a mammoth!"

Surprising Revelation

Despite the fact that the rumbling had momentarily flipped it on its shaggy back, the wolverine was creeping forward behind them. It paused and sniffed the air. The chunky beast would never attack Corey or Lassie while either of them was able to put up a fight, but that black mountain of hair was something else! There was red meat beneath that ancient hair, and the crafty scavenger was very hungry. The wolverine, licking its

Still Being Followed

lips, sat back on its haunches,
fixed its beady eyes on the strange
scene, and waited to see what would
happen next.

What Next?

"Hard as a Rock!"

CHAPTER 2

AN EXCITING DISCOVERY

Corey Stuart kicked the toe of one boot against the dead mammoth's side. "Hard as a rock," he muttered. His heart was pounding with excitement. "Probably been lying there for more than ten thousand years!"

Lassie whined and looked at her master.

"Perfectly preserved in nature's own refrigerator," continued the ranger, trying to roll a rock aside in order to gain a better view of the elephant-size carcass.

Sensing that what they had discovered was important to Corey, Lassie backed off a few paces and sat down respectfully, while the forester thrust his hand excitedly into his warm pocket and pulled out

Lassie Watches

the walkie-talkie. "Hello, Ace. This is Corey again. Do you read me?"

There was no answer.

Corey shuffled slowly around the half-exposed remains. "Too bad its head, trunk, and tusks aren't exposed," he mused to himself. "This way, all I can see is its king-size back." He manipulated the controls of the radio transmitter again. "Ace Dawson, this is Mobile Two talking. Why don't you answer me?"

Corey Calls Ace

"Mobile Two, this is Ace Dawson replying. Are you all right?"

"Of course I'm all right!" answered Stuart. "Why do you ask?"

"Because of the earthquake!" exclaimed the bush pilot. "I could see the earth splitting apart like great jaws. Believe me, friend, it's quite a sight when you're a thousand feet in the air!"

"You don't know what sights *are!*" chided Corey, unable to refrain from ribbing his crony. "That

"Are You All Right?"

little earthquake you enjoyed from
the comfort of your plane just happened to reveal a—"

Before he could utter the word
"mammoth," the ground suddenly
shuddered again, then slammed
back and forth in terrifying
spasms. The hillside erupted like a
volcano, this time spewing forth
the entire body of the enormous
prehistoric beast it had hidden for
so long. Rocks clattered in all directions. Gigantic tree trunks were

Another Tremor

severed. Then the hideous movement ceased as suddenly as it had begun. All was silent . . . except for Corey Stuart.

"My leg," he moaned. "Lassie . . . this rock I'm pinned under has broken my leg!"

Lassie was temporarily stunned by the shock waves that had bounced her up and down. She was unable to respond for an agonizing moment; her mind was a blank. Then, as vision returned to her eyes

Corey Is Hurt

and her mind cleared, she focused anxiously on her master. Corey was crumpled awkwardly beneath a boulder. His pack was split open, and his Mossberg 800 rifle was lying in the snow just inches beyond his reach.

"Lassie! Help me!"

The collie sprang forward, whining piteously, and licked Stuart's taut face.

"Here, girl! Try to dig out some of the ground from under the other

Lassie Wants to Help

end of this rock. Then maybe I'll be able to work up enough leverage to roll it off." Corey winced in pain and pulled his lips tight over his teeth.

Lassie dug desperately at the rock-hard soil—ground that had been frozen for more generations than man can remember. Her efforts were useless, however. Corey realized it would take a bulldozer, or another earthquake, to dent the solid loam.

Desperate Digging

"Forget it, girl," said Corey. "You'll only get bloody feet if you keep that up. Hang on a minute. I'll contact Ace Dawson by walkie-talkie again. He can swing back and scoop us out of here." Grimacing as a sharp pain stabbed through his leg, Corey groped in his pocket for the communication device on which his life depended. When he pulled it out, he stared at it dumbly. The walkie-talkie was smashed.

Useless Walkie-Talkie

Lassie started to dig furiously again.

"No, girl. There are more important things to do than that!" Stuart murmured. The danger of his predicament was slowly coming to him. "Go and fetch me some sticks! I'll have to start a fire before it gets dark, or I'll probably freeze to death."

Lassie stopped digging. The pads on her feet were already scraped raw. She responded instantly to

Lassie Gathers Firewood

Corey's command and scurried off
among the fallen trees, searching
eagerly for suitable branches in the
drifts.

Corey slowly stuffed the shat-
tered fragments of the walkie-
talkie back into his pocket, then
sized up the situation. His attention
was captured by the head of the
long-dead mammoth, which was
so close to him. Its hairy trunk
was coiled stiffly on the snow-cov-
ered rocks, and its enormous ivory

Corey Studies the Situation

tusks curved upward like two fat half-moons. "All I can say," he muttered to himself, "is that I'm glad its eyes aren't open!"

At that moment a cold breeze riffled the stiff black hairs on the beast's bulging forehead, as if in response.

"I've got to contact the curator of the American Museum of Natural History," Corey thought to himself. "If they can remove this specimen intact, and mount it in

What a Specimen!

a below-zero special room, it will become one of the major scientific finds of the century!"

Corey stretched out his arm and attempted to grasp his rifle. It remained out of reach. Then he ran glove-covered fingers over the scattered contents of his pack until he found several cans of K rations. "I may freeze to death, but at least I won't starve to death," he thought gratefully, shifting his position once more.

Corey Reaches for His Gun

Breathing heavily, Lassie was collecting sticks, branches, and shredded sections of bark, neatly depositing all of them at Corey's side. When she had finished, the sun was diving into the frozen silence behind a ragged fringe of distant spruce trees.

"Thanks, girl," Corey said, as he fumbled for his waterproof cylinder of safety matches.

The collie whined anxiously as Stuart cupped a handful of bark

"Thanks, Girl!"

into a pile of tinder, then touched
its edge with a tiny flame. When
sparks caught on and spread them-
selves into a semblance of a campfire, she barked approvingly. She
knew instinctively that she, like the
lean gray wolves who had been her
ancestors, would not freeze in the
snow, but that Corey Stuart could,
even though he was bundled up in
Eskimo clothing.

"Well, girl," said the ranger,
tousling the hair under the collie's

A Warm Fire

long chin, "let's see how things look in the morning." He turned and glanced at his rifle. "Just in case," he added, "would you mind fetching my Mossberg?"

Lassie grasped the heavy rifle between her jaws and dragged it to her master.

"Thanks, Lassie. You're the most reliable companion I've ever had." He smiled at the dog, despite his intense discomfort. "Well, let's get some shut-eye. If the fire burns too

Reliable Companion

low, wake me up!"

The collie nodded her head and stretched out beside the wounded human. Lassie would protect Corey Stuart for she knew he would perish quickly without her.

At the edge of the flickering orange circle fashioned by the guttering flames, the wolverine crouched in straggly shrubbery, waiting impatiently. As soon as both dog and man were asleep, it

Resting

would lunge forward and bury its
teeth in that mountain of red meat
covered with black hair. For a meal
such as that it could afford to wait.

The Wolverine Waits

Undisturbed Silence

CHAPTER 3

ATTACKED BY WOLVES

The mammoth huddled in undisturbed silence throughout the frozen night, its eyes and ears unaware of northern lights dancing in the sky, or the red campfire's fitful crackling. The wolverine, on the other hand, was not silent; its stomach rumbled continually in hunger. It could have attacked the sleeping ranger in its search for flesh, but Lassie, faithfully pacing back and forth like a Marine on sentry duty, was an obstacle not easily overcome.

"Are you all right, girl?" Corey slowly opened his eyes and rolled over on his other side. His back was unbearably stiff from being cramped in the same position all night. He turned his head and

Faithful Sentry

checked the condition of the fire. The collie had apparently dropped fresh twigs on the flame throughout her vigil, for the campfire was burning briskly.

Lassie barked, wagged her tail, and licked Corey's forehead with her tongue.

"Hey! Take it easy!" Stuart exclaimed, grinning through the growing stubble of his beard, despite the fact that sharp fingers of pain were clawing through his

"Take It Easy!"

broken leg again. The grin faded
from his drawn face. "My leg feels
like it's progressing through a
meat grinder. And this rock is as
immovable as ever!"

The weary dog stared at him
with mournful eyes. She did not
comprehend the full meaning of his
words, but she was aware that he
was extremely uncomfortable.

Corey was about to ask her if
she would mind K rations for
breakfast, when crashing sounds

A Painful Situation

in the distant brush caught his attention. The commotion sounded to Corey like a Sherman tank smashing through saplings as though they were matchsticks. But it wasn't the crashing sound that caused the hair on the nape of his neck to prickle, however. It was the accompanying howls that shivered through the air.

"Wolves!" he shouted.

Lassie wheeled about and faced the rock-strewn area where yesterday's earthquake had sprawled

Sounds From the Brush

trees in all directions. While Corey nervously fingered his Mossberg to see if its magazine still held four unfired bullets, the dog explored the wind with her highly sensitive nose. Her quivering nostrils instantly informed her that two types of creatures were approaching with express-train speed . . . and her ears told her that one was being chased, and the other—or others—were in hot pursuit.

"I must say, there's nothing dull

Lassie Senses Danger

about Alaska!" exclaimed Corey, struggling into a sitting position. "I only wish Ace Dawson could see me now. He'll never believe any of this!" He patted the Mossberg's varnished Monte Carlo stock and hefted the six-and-one-half-pound rifle in his hands. Facing in the direction from which the crashing sounds grew ever louder, he added wistfully, "I just hope these bullets are heavy enough to battle with a wolf."

Waiting!

He had barely finished speaking when a bull moose seemed to explode out of nowhere. Its flanks were heaving as it gasped for breath. Its bulging red eyes were glazed with fatigue, and its heavy neck was flecked with foam. The harried creature—larger than a horse—stumbled awkwardly forward, the weight of its enormous antlers apparently dragging down its head. Judging from its bedraggled appearance, Corey estimated

A Bull Moose Appears

it must have run for at least ten
miles without stopping. He raised
the Mossberg to his shoulder and
squinted down the sights. Being
trampled by a tired moose would be
just as unpleasant as being chewed
to death by a pack of wolves, he
decided.

Before he could squeeze the trigger, another spasm of pain ripped
through his leg. He arched backward, accidentally jerking the trigger. A bullet blasted uselessly into

Narrow Escape

the trunk of a nearby tree. Startled by the flash, the noise, and the acrid smoke, the moose leaped over Corey and floundered through a tangle of thicket on the other side of the mammoth.

"What a lousy shot," moaned the ranger, vexed at his pain-induced clumsiness. He forced himself to sit up again and quickly rework the bolt. Then he found himself staring into the faces of three timber wolves.

Further Danger

As Corey adjusted the butt of
his rifle against his right shoulder,
the largest of the wolves took in the
situation at a glance. Here was a
dog-creature, who was snarling at
him like a ferocious fellow carni-
vore; a helpless man-creature with
a gun that spit fire but didn't hit
anything; and a mountain of frozen
flesh covered with long black hair
that stirred restlessly in the icy
wind.

Lassie snarled and bunched her

Lassie Stands Firm

muscles. The fur on her neck bristled.

The wolf wasn't afraid of the dog, but that gun was an object to be treated with respect. Whining a signal to the other two wolves, the leader spun about, and all three of them split up, shifting with the precision of a top-rated football backfield. They were about to execute a maneuver around the hulk of the dead mammoth when Lassie flung herself at them.

The Wolves Shift Positions

"Careful, Lassie. They'll tear you into mincemeat!" croaked Corey, swinging the muzzle of his rifle back and forth, unable to draw an accurate bead on the tumbling bodies that zigzagged back and forth in front of him. He knew that if he squeezed the trigger at the wrong split second, he was just as likely to hit Lassie as he was to drop one of the wolves.

Though outnumbered by the athletic killers she had so recklessly

Lassie Attacks

charged, Lassie easily eliminated
one of the wolves before savage
jaws clamped on her own throat
and she was pulled down into the
trampled snow.

Frightful Sight

Unable to Help

CHAPTER 4

MORE TROUBLE

"Lassie!" cried Corey in an agonized voice as he frantically thrashed back and forth in an effort to tear his leg free from the heavy rock that pinned him to the ground. The blood drained from his haggard cheeks as he watched his ever

faithful pet wrestle with the sur-
viving wolves. Just as the wolves
were about to get the best of her,
the ranger managed to line one of
them up in his gunsights. His index
finger closed on the trigger, and a
bullet lodged in the wolf's skull.
The other lobo released its grip,
panted balefully for a moment,
then slunk into the underbrush, its
tail between its legs.

"Lassie!"

The collie did not move.

The Last of the Lobos

Corey painfully stretched out his arm, vainly attempting to touch her with his gloved fingertips. "Girl! Girl!"

The collie lay motionless in the snow. A dark pool of blood stained the icy ground beneath her throat.

An ordinary observer would have reeled back in horror at the sight of two dead wolves, a mummified mammoth, and a dog who was obviously bleeding to death. But the wolverine, who had safely studied

Corey Stretches Toward Lassie

the struggle from the sidelines, was
no run-of-the-mill observer. He
knew that with the dog dead, the
crippled man-creature would fall
easy prey to a quick attack from
behind, and he would then have
enough flesh to eat for a very long
time. Prodded by a particularly intense hunger pang, the wolverine
started to inch forward when the
collie moved her head.

"Lassie! Can you hear me?"

The dog moaned piteously and

The Wolverine Approaches

attempted to wag her tail.

"Try to crawl to me, girl. Try to crawl to me!"

Corey stretched out his arm again. As he did so, he was suddenly aware of a brown shape plunging toward him from the rear. He twisted around with lightning speed and fired point-blank at the wolverine without attempting to aim. The bullet whistled harmlessly over the animal's head, but the powder flash which seared its

Corey Fires

face made the animal skid to a halt.
For what seemed like an eternity,
wounded man and treacherous
beast stared at one another, while
Stuart fumbled with the bolt. Then,
before he could fire again, the wolverine melted back out of sight.

"That means there's only one
bullet left in the magazine," muttered Corey to himself, half-
stunned by the dizzying succession
of violent events. "My extra bullets
were scattered in the snow when

"Only One Bullet Left!"

the pack split open. One more knock-down, drag-out fight like this, and my rifle will be as useless as a rolled-up newspaper." He squinted bleary eyes toward the thicket into which the wolverine had vanished. "I'm not a gambling man, but I'll wager my life that that monster will be back as soon as I'm asleep, or too weak to defend myself."

A heartbreaking whine brought tears to his eyes. Turning his head,

Lassie Whimpers

he watched with parted lips as Lassie attempted to hitch herself toward him on her belly.

"Come on, girl. You can make it! Don't give up now!"

The collie feebly wagged her tail once more, then slumped forward until her narrow chin flopped heavily on the leather boot of Corey's free leg.

"There, there, girl. I'll fix that wound."

Lacking a bandage, he scooped

"Come On, Girl!"

up a handful of cold snow and pressed it against the jagged gashes on her throat. Stuart examined the lacerations carefully. The teeth of both wolves had torn her regal neck, but luckily had not sliced through the artery, windpipe, or pulsating jugular vein. "You'll be all right, girl. *You'll be all right!* Just rest your head here on my lap." Tears streaked his cheeks as he gently ran trembling fingers through the long golden hair that

"You'll Be All Right!"

hung so listlessly on her neck. After a while—he had no idea how much time had elapsed—she appeared to fall asleep.

Lassie Sleeps

Consciousness Returns

CHAPTER 5

LASSIE RECOVERS

When Lassie regained consciousness several hours later, she moaned softly, raised her head, and slowly parted her eyelids. She felt as weak as a newborn puppy from loss of blood. She knew that her strength was returning, however.

The icy snow Corey had packed
against her throat had stopped the
bleeding and soothed the wound.

Noting that she had awakened,
the ranger stroked the short white
fur under her chin. "Thank heavens
you're going to be all right," he
murmured.

The collie turned her aristocratic
head and saw that the campfire she
had kept blazing so faithfully had
collapsed into a heap of gray ashes.

"The fire's gone out, girl,"

Lassie Is All Right

mumbled Stuart. "When your strength comes back, I think you'd better fetch some more wood. If I stay warm, I can keep alive until Ace Dawson returns with his plane at the end of the week. Don't overdo it, though. Just bring me some small sticks."

Lassie rose unsteadily to her feet. She sniffed the cold ashes and slowly wagged her tail. She hadn't understood every word her master had spoken, but she knew he wanted

A Cold Fire

her to get more firewood. Licking his bewhiskered cheek with her tongue, she turned, shook the shaggy hair on her shoulders, and stumbled toward the thicket—the thicket in which the wolverine crouched waiting.

The beast drew back behind a tree trunk as it watched her coming. It would wait until she passed, then craftily follow her and seize her from behind. A single swift movement would leave her kicking

Crafty Observer

helplessly on the ground. Killing her would simply be a matter of reopening that healing gash on her throat. The wolves may have muffed the job, but the wolverine would not.

Lassie didn't see the thickset creature as she limped past. And because the wind was blowing in the opposite direction, her sensitive nose failed to pick up its scent. Since wolverines are virtually extinct in most of North America,

Lassie Limps Past

she knew nothing about the habits
of this despised cabin-invader and
trap-line robber. She had no idea
that a wolverine is the largest mem-
ber of the bloodthirsty weasel fam-
ily, and is not related in any way
to the timber wolves with whom she
had just tangled. She didn't know
that a full-grown wolverine is
plucky enough, at times, to bluff
even a grizzly bear away from a
carcass.

As the collie stumbled past the

Unaware of Danger

tree trunk and headed for a nearby fallen aspen whose smaller
branches looked as though they
could be snapped off, the wolverine
rose stealthily and plodded along
behind her, carefully raising and
lowering its padded feet so as to
make no sound.

Lassie Is Followed

Corey Waits Patiently

CHAPTER 6

EXIT ONE WOLVERINE

Unaware of the drama that was about to take place, Corey Stuart shifted his position under the rock again, rested his Mossberg 800 rifle on his lap, and glanced up at the frozen mammoth. "Here's to you, mammoth!" he said, smiling wryly in spite of his predicament. "Do you mind if I open a can of K rations?"

The mammoth made no response.

Peeling off the cover of the small, flat can, the forest ranger, wretchedly cold, jerked off his gloves and removed the contents of the container with numb fingertips. He wolfed down the morsels hungrily, then pulled his gloves back on. "I wonder how cold it is?" he muttered.

K Ration Lunch

While Corey struggled into a more comfortable position, Lassie seized one of the branches of the aspen tree and tried to shake it loose. Although she swung her head back and forth, it would not break free. She tried another branch, and failed again. The tree had been felled by the earthquake, and it was still green and moist inside.

The wolverine watched her with beady eyes, waiting for his chance.

Sensing that she would have to

Struggle With a Branch

uncover a long-dead tree whose
branches would crack off with little
effort, the collie clambered over the
aspen's trunk and continued her
search. It had been easier to find
dead branches yesterday, for then
she had been picking up debris that
was within easy reach on top of
the covering snow. Since—with the
efficiency of a vacuum cleaner—
she had picked the immediate vicinity completely clean of sticks, today
she would have to range farther

Lassie Goes On

and farther afield.

Twitching its lower lip back and
forth, the wolverine silently padded
behind Lassie as she zigzagged toward the frozen riverbank, near
Bear Skull Point. It was on the flat
expanse of this wide body of water
that her master's bush pilot friend
was to land his plane when Corey's
seven-day vacation was up. The
banks of the winding river, which
was as smooth as a dance floor,
were literally bristling with dead

Firewood Bonanza

twigs and branches. Panting happily, and sensing that her strength was surging back, the collie seized the nearest branch with her teeth. It was then that the wolverine struck.

Had Lassie not slipped on the ice as she struggled with the branch, the wolverine's lunge would have knocked her sprawling. As it was, the starving beast's wedge-shaped head glanced off her flank, its canine teeth ripping a

The Wolverine Strikes

long red streak in her side. Startled,
Lassie let the branch drop and
threw herself to one side like a
boxer skillfully outstepping his op-
ponent. The wolverine slid for
twenty feet on the glossy ice, twirl-
ing around three times, before it
braked to a halt. Snarling with fury
and frustration, the animal regained its balance and lunged for
the collie again. This time, it de-
termined, it would not miss.

But it did. Lassie was more agile

Lassie Sidesteps

than her low-slung foe. It was as though a heavyweight boxer were attacking a graceful ballerina. Effortlessly flinging herself to one side again, her anger reaching the boiling point because of the fresh wound in her side, Lassie watched her bewildered assailant lose its balance for the second time. The wolverine slid awkwardly across the ice and crashed headlong into a rock that bulged from the white shoreline.

Awkward Slide

After a stunned moment the animal rose to its feet and wheeled about, focusing glittery eyes on its prey. To its annoyance, Lassie had backed away, and now appeared to be executing a strange dance on a section of paper-thin ice. Curling back its upper lip in a snarl of hate, the beast grunted hideously and lunged forward for the third time. It was unaware that the ice under the dancing collie was dangerously thin.

Furious Wolverine

One of Lassie's rear feet plunged through the ice just as the wolverine reached her. The collie scrambled to one side and flung herself on a pancake of thicker ice. From there she clawed her way to safety. When she looked back she saw a huge splash. The wolverine had fallen through the ice. For a moment her eyes were able to follow the struggling form as it tried mightily to batter its way out of the icy water. Then it was swept under.

Through the Ice

Lassie barked a satisfied bark and returned to her job of hunting firewood. She must get wood back for a fire or Corey would freeze to death.

Back to Work

"What Happened?"

CHAPTER 7

A SMALL VISITOR

"What happened to your side?"
Corey queried anxiously as Lassie
dragged a heavy branch into the
clearing and deposited it with a
thump on the pile of gray ashes,
scattering them in all directions.
"Did you tangle with another—"

Corey was about to say "wolf," when he realized what had happened. "The *wolverine* did that!" he exclaimed.

The collie barked "yes" in answer.

"Did you kill it?"

Corey twisted and stared into the underbrush, his rifle cocked and ready, as though expecting the thickset glutton to make a final curtain call. He knew instinctively, however, that the animal was no

Corey Is Alert

longer anywhere near.

Once more Lassie barked her response. Stuart had been with her for so many years that he immediately knew she was saying "yes" again.

"Good girl! I should say, good grief! You've really had your share of adventure since we arrived in this place!" He narrowed his eyes and stared at his pet in wonder.

Flattered at the respectful tone

"Good Girl!"

of his voice, Lassie shook her head
self-consciously, then turned and
trotted back toward the riverbank.
It would take more than one dead
branch to keep a fire going.

Unaware that he was being
watched in wide-eyed wonder by a
small figure who peered around the
flank of the dead mammoth, Corey
glanced at the two dead wolves and
softly exclaimed, "This place sure
is a mess. And I always prided
myself on being such a neat

Back for More Fuel

camper! Of course, I don't normally sit in wet snow with one of my legs crushed under a boulder!"

The Tlingit Indian boy, who had been watching Corey's every movement for ten minutes, sucked in his breath as the forest ranger flicked open his waterproof match cylinder and expertly ignited the shredded end of the branch. The boy's father had no such container. As a matter of fact, the boy's father never used matches on his hunting excursions;

Surprised Observer

he had found flint and steel more reliable.

"That's more like it," sighed Corey as the heat from the flickering flame caressed his haggard face. He rubbed the back of his wrist against the stubble on his chin. "I must look like the *before* photograph in a razor-blade advertisement!"

He was about to prod the fire once more when another spasm shot through his leg. He arched

"That's Better!"

backward in pain. Stretched flat on his back in the snow, he stared straight into the eyes of the eight-year-old Indian boy, who had finally crept forward, overcome with curiosity.

"Where did *you* come from? Or am I having hallucinations?"

The boy took two steps backward, spun around, and scurried off.

"Wait! Come back!" pleaded Corey, sitting up again as the pain

"Where Did You Come From?"

in his leg subsided.

At that moment Lassie burst into the clearing, proudly dragging another dead branch.

"After him, girl!" shouted Corey, waving wildly in the direction of his vanished visitor. "There's a little Indian boy over there! Maybe he can persuade his parents to roll this rock off my leg." Wracked by another wave of pain, Corey lurched sideways. His movement knocked the crackling branch

"Follow Him, Lassie!"

out of its bed of ashes. Orange
flames from the branch leaped to
the piece of wood Lassie had just
brought; they nibbled eagerly at
the shaggy bark. The intense pain
had become too severe. Corey was
knocked unconscious.

Lassie dashed around to the far
side of the silent mammoth and
paced back and forth like a leopard
in a cage, nervously sniffing the
ground. In an instant she picked up
the fresh scent. She quickly bounded

Lassie Picks Up the Scent

off through a network of fallen trees. The frightened youngster had left an easy trail to follow. His tiny moccasins made crystal-clear marks in the powdery snow.

In the deserted clearing behind Lassie, near the unconscious figure of her master, flames from the second burning branch stretched out hungry fingers and touched the dry base of a nearby thicket.

A Clear Trail

Frightened Indian Boy

CHAPTER 8

STRANGE PEOPLE

Twisting and turning between endless tree trunks, which had been knocked topsy-turvy by the earthquake, the Indian boy floundered toward the winter hunting hut of his parents. On the way he smashed headlong into his little sister, who had secretly followed him, though expressly forbidden to do so.

"Out of my way, Little Salmon!" shouted the boy. "I have something I must tell Father!"

"Wait for me, White Bear!" squealed the girl, picking herself up off the snow.

The boy paused and shot her a withering glance. "You weren't supposed to follow me! Don't you know that we men like to be alone? How can I ever become a mighty

"Out of My Way!"

hunter with *you* tagging along in my footsteps from morning till night?"

"I can hunt just as well as you can!" retorted the girl, her pride injured. "Mother said so!" She stuck out her tongue.

White Bear was about to exclaim "Aw-w-w-w . . . squaws!" when Lassie soared over a fallen log and landed between the two youngsters.

Startled by the unexpected appearance of a kind of dog they had

"I Can Hunt as Well as You!"

never seen before, both children pulled back in fear. Lassie wagged her tail pleadingly and whined at them. Because the collie wanted the boy to follow her back to the clearing where Corey Stuart lay helplessly pinned to the frozen ground, she stretched her pointed head forward, parted her jaws slightly, and seized him firmly by the front of his loose fur jacket. Thinking the dog was about to attack him in the manner of the half-wild huskies,

Lassie Wants Help

White Bear pummeled Lassie on her head and neck with gloved fists.

"She isn't going to bite you!" shrieked Little Salmon, thrusting her tiny frame gamely between dog and boy.

Lassie released her grip on the boy's parka. She was hurt and puzzled by his hostile reaction.

"How do *you* know!" challenged the boy, trying to recover his composure. "I was bitten three times by the last sled dog Father had—

"She Won't Hurt You!"

before a Kodiak bear carried it off."

"And now we don't have *any!*" mourned the girl, trying to remember how many times her brother had actually been attacked by dogs that were half wolf.

"Oh, yes, we do!" replied White Bear, examining Lassie in a new light.

The girl read his mind. "Oh! Won't Father be proud when we bring *this* dog to him?"

Unable to understand a single

"We'll Take Her to Father!"

word of their odd verbal exchange, Lassie wheeled away from the youngsters and retraced her steps hesitantly. She paused frequently and whined an urgent invitation for them to follow.

"She wants us to follow her!" ventured the girl.

"No, I want *her* to follow *us!*" corrected the boy.

"Silence!" rasped a hoarse voice. A spasm of coughing followed. "Do you wretched offspring have to

"She Wants Us to Follow Her!"

bark like seals all the time?"

"Father ... *look!*" growled White Bear, endeavoring to make his voice rumble from his chest in the manner of the elder males of his tribe. He pointed at Lassie.

The middle-aged Tlingit hunter stared at the collie through narrow slits in his wooden snow goggles. He coughed again, then craftily rubbed the back of one tattered glove against his straggly black moustache. Waving a harpoon-like

"Father . . . Look!"

device with the other hand, he gestured for both youngsters to close their mouths.

Unaware of his complete indifference to dogs as companions, Lassie approached him, lowered her head, and barked several times. Then she whined and retraced her steps. Surely *he* would understand and follow!

"That's no sled dog," the Indian muttered finally, half under his breath. "That's the kind of dog that

"That's No Sled Dog!"

tastes good in a stew pot . . . and I haven't had a chunk of good dog meat for more moons than I care to remember!"

"What's that smoke over there?" asked the little girl, pointing toward several black wisps slowly curling skyward in the distance.

"Never mind the smoke!" grunted her father. "Stay here and watch the dog while I return to the hut and get my rope."

"Father wants to eat the dog!"

"What's That Smoke?"

exclaimed Little Salmon. "Do you think he'll let us have a bite?"

"Of course!" replied her brother, watching the collie closely so she wouldn't escape. "Father always lets us eat dog meat!"

Watching Lassie

Lassie Is Caught

CHAPTER 9

THE FIRE SPREADS

Choking and gasping because of the noose the Tlingit had slipped over her unsuspecting head when he returned from the hut, Lassie lunged backward with such force that the other end of the rope pulled free of the Indian's hands, and the frayed slipknot tore open.

Muttering an explosive series of oaths, the Indian scrambled after the end of the rope on his hands and knees. Then, suddenly roaring with anger, he picked up his harpoon-like device and heaved it after the fleeing collie.

As the stubby iron head of the weapon dug into the bark behind her, Lassie cleared the fallen log she had soared over when first confronting the children. She would

Fleeing Collie

have spun about and attacked the Indian, as she had attacked the wolves, but she didn't want to waste time. Corey Stuart had ordered her to go for help, and these strangely dressed people with bronze skin obviously weren't going to be of much aid.

"Don't kill her, Father!" screamed the little girl, who had suddenly decided she didn't want to eat Lassie after all.

"Why not?" the frustrated

"Don't Kill Her!"

man rasped. He would have vaulted over the log in hot pursuit of Lassie had he not been stopped in his tracks by a seizure of violent coughing.

"Because I want her!" answered the little girl defiantly. "I want to play with her!" Turning her back on her father and brother, she scrambled after the dog.

"Shall I stop her?" asked the boy.

"No," muttered his father. "Let her go. I will punish her when she

The Girl Follows Lassie

returns to the hut."

Stumbling after the dog proved more difficult than Little Salmon had thought. Lassie's footprints dodged back and forth in the powdery snow, and sometimes disappeared altogether when the dog would leap a fallen tree trunk. The girl was about to give up and turn back when she caught sight of something ahead. She twisted her mouth into an "I told you so!" expression. She *had* been right about

A Fearful Sight

those black wisps curling toward the sky. There *was* a fire ahead of her!

Wheezing because of the ever-increasing smoke, she shuffled forward a few more steps until she broke through a line of uprooted underbrush at the edge of a rocky clearing. Though she was normally afraid of nothing except her father's wrath, the sight that met her eyes caused her to recoil in fear. Peeking through her fingers, she

Frightened

drank in the details of the scene before her. Then she turned and fled in the direction of her parents' hut.

Corey Stuart stirred and opened his eyes. Immediately he shrank against the rock that mercilessly held him prisoner. A blast of heat from a score of blazing tree trunks seemed to be consuming him like a roast on a spit. So unbearable was the intensity of the heat that the skin on his lips began to crack.

Intense Heat

"Lassie!" he shouted as the dog dashed up to him and yanked desperately at his parka. "Go away before you're destroyed!"

While knot after knot in the crackling tree trunks exploded like a series of small hand grenades, the mammoth suddenly seemed to stir with life. Heat waves from the burning trees fanned the long black hair on its ears until the ears actually appeared to move. A rock collapsed beneath its trunk, and the

The Mammoth Catches Fire

trunk seemed to writhe like a giant snake. Then a clump of burning ashes ignited the mammoth's back, and in an instant the entire mountain of flesh and hair was burning.

"Oh, no!" moaned Corey, temporarily forgetting that he was likely to share the mammoth's fate. "There goes one of the greatest scientific finds the world has ever known." All that protruded now from the swirling mass of flames were two white tusks which curved

"Oh, No!"

upward in the smoke. Then they broke off and sank into the melting snow beneath. In moments every last visage of the great beast had disappeared.

The Mammoth Is Destroyed

Ace Hears the News

CHAPTER 10

RESCUED

"What do you mean, a forest fire has been reported in the vicinity of Bear Skull Point!" queried Ace Dawson as he leaped lightly from his twin-engined plane at the ranger station airstrip near Red Dog Pass. "This is winter time, not fire season. I just left that area, and the only thing I saw was a Grade-B earthquake!"

"Apparently the quake knocked down a lot of dry timber. I've dispatched several helicopters to the scene with smoke jumpers and full equipment," snapped the assistant district ranger. Vapor from his breath hung heavy in the frosty air. "And that was no Grade-B earthquake, old boy. Those ground tremors really shook that region!"

"I Saw a Small Earthquake!"

Dawson grabbed the ranger by the shoulder. "Wait a minute! As you know, Corey Stuart is looking over some possible wilderness sites near Bear Skull Point! He told me to pick him up at the end of the week!"

"I'll bet you a month's pay there won't be anything left to pick up except a handful of ashes," mumbled the ranger, turning away to hide his concern.

"You don't know Corey Stuart!"

"Corey Is Up There!"

shouted Dawson. His face was flushed. "*Nothing* can give a knockout punch to that fellow. He's as rugged as they come."

"We'll know shortly," answered the worried ranger as he pulled open the door to the small headquarters building. "My smoke jumpers will soon be calling in by walkie-talkie. Care to stick around and see what happens?"

"Not on your life!" bellowed Dawson. He spun on his heels and

"We'll Have a Report Shortly!"

sprinted toward his plane. "I've got landing skis on this plane, and I'm going back right now."

Unaware that smoke jumpers had landed on the frozen river and were already clambering up the snow-crusted banks with fire-fighting equipment, Corey moaned, "You certainly are a sight for sore eyes!" as the ragged-looking Tlingit Indian, his wife, and two children trotted toward him across the

"I'm Going Back!"

smoke-clogged clearing.

Recognizing the man as the one who had tried to strangle her, Lassie flattened back her ears and snarled.

"Down, girl!" commanded Stuart. "I think they've come to help me."

Drenched with perspiration because of the heat, the four Indians leaned hard against the rock, grunting with effort as they tried to move it. After a few moments

Help Had Arrived

the little girl, too small to be of any use in the pushing effort, turned away from the others and patted Corey on the head as though she were trying to comfort a tiny puppy with a thorn in his foot.

"Can't move it!" muttered the Indian. He coughed violently and shrank away from the heat of the burning trees.

Corey couldn't understand what he was saying, but he could tell from the tone of the man's voice

Little Salmon Comforts Corey

that he was about to give up.

"I'll give you this rifle if you'll remove this miserable rock!" pleaded the ranger, holding up his Mossberg. Sweat was pouring down his face.

The Tlingit examined the gun with greedy eyes and babbled a few words to his wife. Then they pushed against the rock again. Slowly the boulder shifted its position.

"Move over! We'll help you do it!" Two smoke jumpers arrived at

About to Give Up

that moment and hurried forward
to lend a hand. Lassie jumped up
and down, barking frantically.
Staring at them as though they
were apparitions, the Tlingit and
his squaw pulled away.

"Join the party!" laughed Corey
through split lips. He was begin-
ning to feel lightheaded. "Say,
where did *you* come from?"

"Never mind the comic strip
chitchat," muttered one of them
through his protective face shield.

Smoke Jumpers

"We've got to get you out from under this rock and over to Bear Skull Point. It's the only spot where a plane can get in to get you out of here."

Using their special shovels as levers, they deftly forced the rock off Corey's leg.

"Look at that!" exclaimed one of the smoke jumpers. "It's swollen to twice its normal size! It must really have given him pain."

Stuart glanced down at his leg.

They Work Quickly

"Looks like something out of a horror movie!" he said in a matter-of-fact manner.

"How come there are two dead wolves over there?" asked one of the smoke jumpers as he and the other jumper positioned the ranger on a makeshift stretcher they had fashioned out of shovel handles.

"It's a long story," began Corey. "But it's not the wolves that matter . . . it's that mammoth over there!"

"Let's Go!"

"*What* mammoth?" exclaimed one of the jumpers.

"Humor him," murmured the other. "He's probably delirious from the pain."

Corey Stuart closed his eyes and decided not to pursue the subject. Just at that moment Ace Dawson's familiar voice rang out, "Follow me, fellows. My plane's waiting for him right over there on the river!"

The ranger opened his eyes again. "Hey, what are *you* doing

"Over Here, Fellows!"

here so soon? You weren't supposed to come after me until the end of the week!"

Dawson chucked him under the chin. "I got worried about you! After all, I leave you for a day and a half, and what do you do? You start two earthquakes and light a spectacular forest fire!"

"Let me tell you about the mammoth," murmured Corey. "You've got to go back and get that mammoth's tusks!"

Ace Greets Corey

"Sure, sure," said Ace. "I'll have Lassie tell me all about it!"

As the plane skidded down the length of the frozen river, coughed, and took off, Corey insisted, "I tell you, there *was* a mammoth down there! The fire destroyed it!"

"Well, there's nothing in that clearing now except embers and ashes!" replied Ace. "Am I right, Lassie?"

The collie barked happily, over-joyed that her master was safe

Ready to Take Off

again. She had already forgotten
about the prehistoric beast that had
been exposed by the earthquake.

Ace Dawson turned and glanced
at his friend. Corey was sound
asleep. Ace grinned and headed for
the distant ranger station airstrip.
He'd fly Corey back to look for
those tusks another day.

"We'll Be Back!"

Other BIG LITTLE BOOKS Available

WHITMAN *Big Book Adventures*

Based on famous TV shows

I SPY

THE GREEN HORNET

THE MAN FROM U.N.C.L.E.

BONANZA

LASSIE

FLIPPER

THE BIG VALLEY

PATTY DUKE

GILLIGAN'S ISLAND

VOYAGE TO THE BOTTOM OF THE SEA